THE MAGICIAN'S BOY

SUSAN COOPER

THE MAGICIAN'S BOY

• • •

illustrated by Serena Riglietti

Aladdin Paperbacks • NEW YORK   LONDON   TORONTO   SYDNEY

THE MAGICIAN'S BOY

ONE

There was once a Boy who worked for a Magician. Every day he polished the Magician's magic wands and the gold stars and moons on his great blue robe. He weeded the garden where the magic herbs grew, and crushed their seeds into powder for the Magician's spells. He worked very hard indeed. But he wasn't happy.

More than anything in the world, the Boy wanted to learn magic—but the Magician would not teach him.

The Boy fed the six white rabbits that lived in a hutch in the garden, but he was always startled when he saw the Magician pull one of them out of somebody's hat. He washed the dishes in the kitchen, and watched enviously when the Magician picked up an empty jug and poured milk out of it. How did he do these things?

"Master," he begged, "teach me! Teach me magic!"

But the Magician always said, "Not yet,

Boy. Not till the time is right. Not yet."

When the Magician went out to perform, the Boy went with him, to help him on stage, and to catch any rabbits he might pull out of hats. The Boy loved those days, because then he had one really special job too.

When the Magician performed, he always took with him a little puppet theatre in which he showed the play "Saint George and the Dragon"—and the Boy was allowed to oper-ate the puppets. The Boy stood on a box behind the tiny stage, hidden by a curtain, and he pulled the puppets' strings while the Magician told the story of the play.

It was an odd little play. One of the people in it was Father Christmas, but all he had to do was introduce the other characters to the audience. These were the wicked Dragon, who loved fighting; the Turkish Knight, who fought the Dragon but could never beat him; and the Doctor, who was there in case anyone was wounded. And of course there was the hero, Saint George.

The Boy was especially proud of the way he made Saint George kill the Dragon, at the end. The wounded Dragon staggered round in a circle, puffed out three clouds of white smoke, jumped up in the air and fell down dead. (The white smoke was really chalk dust, puffed by the Boy from a little pipe.) The watching children always cheered at this, so the Boy was pleased. It wasn't magic, but it was the next best thing.

One Christmas, the Magician and the Boy went to perform at a family party given by a Mr. and Mrs. Pennywinkle, in a grand stone house as big as a castle.

"Mr. Pennywinkle is a very important person!" said the Magician, frowning at the Boy. "Everything must be *perfect*!"

The Magician was a very tall man, with a beaky nose, black eyebrows like doormats,

and a bristly mustache. He was alarming when he frowned.

The Boy said, "Yes, Master! Of course!" He gave the magic wands an extra polish, he shampooed the rabbits, and he repainted the trees on the back wall of the puppet theatre stage.

And off they went to the party.

TWO

At the party, Mr. and Mrs. Pennywinkle's house was full of light and music, and the Magician's audience was full of children. They gasped and clapped at the Magician's tricks, especially when he took six eggs one by one out of Mr. Pennywinkle's bow tie, broke them into Mrs. Pennywinkle's purse, pulled out a Christmas cake and showed the purse to be perfectly empty, clean and dry.

I wish I could do that! thought the Boy, as he swept up the eggshells.

But it was time for the play.

"Now for the terrifying story of 'Saint George and the Dragon'!" boomed the Magician, and he pulled back the curtain covering the stage of the little theatre. Behind the stage the Boy stood, hidden, ready to pull the puppets' strings.

"To begin, let us meet our characters!" cried the Magician. "First—Father Christmas!"

The children all cheered, as the unseen Boy made the fat little Father Christmas puppet turn head over heels onstage, and bow to them.

"The Dragon!"

Quickly the Boy hung the Father Christmas puppet on his hook, and took the bright green Dragon from the row of hanging puppets. He pulled the strings to make the Dragon run onstage.

The children shouted and hissed. The Boy made the Dragon open its fearsome red jaws at them, and huff out a puff of white smoke.

The children howled with joy.

"Saint George!" cried the Magician, and the Boy hastily hung up the Dragon puppet and reached for the bold little figure of Saint George, with his sword and shield, and the red cross on his white tunic.

But the Saint George puppet wasn't there.

The other puppets all hung from their strings behind the stage, waiting. There was Father Christmas, and the Turkish Knight with his curving sword, and the black-coated Doctor. But there was no Saint George.

The Boy looked round, in panic.

"SAINT GEORGE!" roared the Magician impatiently.

The Boy was terrified. He stepped out from behind the theatre and stood there shaking. "I'm sorry, Master," he said in a very small voice, "Saint George seems to be missing."

The children all booed loudly.

The Magician looked down with eyes so angry that the Boy was afraid he would turn him into a rabbit. The Magician's tall figure seemed to grow and grow, towering over the Boy, and he pointed a long finger at him.

"Then you must find him!" he hissed. The finger came very close, with its long sharp nail. "You will go where you must go,

through all the Land of Story, until you find Saint George!"

He swung his arm so that his long dark-blue sleeve swung past the Boy's face, and the Boy saw gold moons and stars flash by, and felt himself falling, falling. . . .

THREE

The Boy fell to the ground and opened his eyes.

The Magician and the children were gone. He seemed to be in a wood. The trees all looked oddly round and stiff, like the trees he had painted on the back wall of the stage.

And standing around him he saw, to his amazement, the puppets from his play: Father Christmas, the Turkish Knight, the

Doctor, and the Dragon. But they weren't puppets now. They were alive, and bigger than he was himself.

The Dragon was *much* bigger. He opened his red jaws and roared, with a far more impressive puff of smoke than the Boy ever gave him. Father Christmas, the Turkish Knight and the Doctor all screamed, and ran away. The Dragon ran after them, chasing them into the wood, roaring.

The Boy was left alone, staring around. Where was he?

He heard a cough. It seemed to come from behind the nearest tree. He went to look, and found a low wooden signpost. Its two arms

pointed in opposite directions, and there were words painted on them.

The words said:

Only a child can find the way
To bring Saint George back to the play.

The Boy read this to himself, twice.

"Well, that's no help!" he said, and he turned away to look for a path through the wood.

"Hey!" said a voice.

The Boy turned. He could see nothing but the signpost. "Where are you?" he said. "Who is it?"

"I'm here!" said the voice. It was a gruff little voice. It sounded cross.

Suddenly the Boy saw that the signpost was jumping up and down. It had two short legs, with large feet, wearing boots.

"You can talk!" he said.

"I know that," said the signpost. "But can you read?"

"Of course I can," said the Boy. He pointed to the words on the signpost, and read them aloud:

"Only a child can find the way
To bring Saint George back to the play."

"There you are then," said the signpost. It bounced up and down on its two little legs, and clicked its boots together.

"That's useless," the Boy said. "It doesn't tell me where the way *is*."

"Use your head," said the signpost. "You're in the Land of Story. You have to travel through stories."

"What stories?" said the Boy.

"The ones you've been told all your life, of course," said the signpost. "Starting with nursery rhymes. Choose a nursery rhyme. Come on. Any rhyme."

The Boy's mind went blank. "Er," he said.

"Er . . . the Old Woman Who Lived in a Shoe."

"Not a great choice," said the signpost. "She doesn't get out much. Still, here we go." And it went trotting off through the trees.

FOUR

The signpost trotted on through the trees. They looked like green lollipops.

The Boy followed, because he didn't know what else to do. They came to an open space, and in it was a gigantic shoe, as big as a house. It was a real shoe, made of leather, with huge shoelaces, but there were windows set neatly into its sides. Just over the heel there was a front door, with steps leading up to it.

Over the top of the shoe, where a foot would go in, was a sturdy tiled roof, with a smoking chimney. The Boy thought the house looked more like a boot than a shoe, but nobody had ever told him a story about the Old Woman Who Lived in a Boot.

The signpost gave a loud whistle, and out of the front door came a yelling crowd of children, jumping and quarrelling. Some were barefoot, some were only half dressed, some were very grubby. Some swung on the giant shoelaces, some pointed at the Boy and giggled.

The Old Woman came running down the steps after them, very cross, shouting, "Hannah, Ellie, Marina, get off those laces! Jack, Charlie, Liam, put some clothes on!"

She stopped, drying her hands on her apron. She wasn't so very old, the Boy saw— just tired.

"Oh dear," she said to herself, "it's a hard thing to be blessed with so many little darlings."

The Boy said, "Excuse me, ma'am—"

She looked at him in horror. "Oh no!" she

said. "I'm sorry, not another child! I simply cannot cope! Try another shoe—a size larger!"

Three little girls came grabbing at her apron, teasing, laughing.

"I don't want a home, ma'am," the Boy said. "I'm just looking for Saint George."

The Old Woman tried to keep her balance, swatting at her children. "Well, you won't find him here—there's not a man in the land who would take on a family this size. Not even a saint!"

The other children came running, shouting.

"Can you tell me where to find Saint

George?" the Boy yelled, as a small boy climbed up his back.

The Old Woman didn't answer. She shook herself free of the giggling children. "Quiet, all of you! Oh, what shall I do? For two pins I'd whip you all soundly and put you to bed!"

The Boy thought that sounded like a good idea—but then he heard music. So did the children. They all stopped jumping about, and listened.

Out of the trees came a cheerful tune, coming closer, closer—and into the clearing came a tall thin man playing a pipe. He wore pants and a shirt patched with red and blue and yellow, and shoes to match.

"Oh dear oh dear," said the signpost. It jumped up and down at the Boy's feet. "You know who that is?" it said.

The Boy said, "He looks like the Pied Piper of Hamelin."

"He is," the signpost said. "And now we're in trouble."

FIVE

The children began skipping in time to the Piper's tune, clustering around him, laughing. The Piper kept on walking, so they skipped after him, out of the clearing, through the wood.

"Children!" called the Old Woman. "Come back!"

But the children all skipped on, and the Boy went with them. The music was so happy that his feet wanted to skip too. The signpost came with him, but it was not at all happy. It kept muttering in its gruff little voice, "Oh dear, oh dear, oh dear."

Through the trees the children went, dancing to the Piper's music, and the path began to rise steeply. Up and up they went, until they were on a stony mountain, high above the wood.

Far below, the Boy could see the Shoe in its clearing. The Old Woman was running to and fro, flapping her apron, calling, "Children! Come back!"

Ahead of him on the path, the Boy heard a great creaking sound, and in the side of the mountain, a big door began to open. The Piper headed for it, playing merrily, leading the children in. The Boy ran after him.

"Sir," he called, "you can't do this! These are not Hamelin children, they belong to the Old Woman. She hasn't done you any harm, you can't take her family away!"

The Piper stopped playing, and looked down at the Boy. He was a very good player, but he didn't look very smart.

"These children aren't from Hamelin?" he said.

"No!" said the Boy. "They live in a shoe."

"What a ridiculous place to live," said the Piper, and he put his pipe to his lips again and went on into the mountain, leading the skipping children through the big door.

"Come back!" called the Boy, but the door slammed shut. Behind him, the Boy heard a wail, and he turned, to see the youngest of the old Woman's children, a very small girl who hadn't been able to keep up with the rest. She toddled up to the door, crying. "Want to go too!" she sobbed.

"What's your name?" said the Boy.

"Zoe," said the little one, and howled.

"Well, come on, Zoe," said the Boy. "Let's

see if this mountain has a back door!" And he tucked small Zoe under his arm and ran as fast as he could along the path round the base of the mountain. The signpost thudded along after him, puffing.

Sure enough, there was another door at the back of the mountain, set into the rock. Faint sounds of music came from behind it, growing louder, and suddenly the door swung open. Out came the Piper, piping, with the children skipping after him.

Zoe gave a squeal of joy, and wriggled out of the Boy's arms and ran to join them.

"Quick!" said the Boy. He grabbed the

signpost and stood it on the path, so that one of its arms was hidden in a holly bush and the other pointed back the way they had come.

The Pied Piper didn't notice what the Boy had done. Lost in his music, he glanced at the pointing arm and followed its pointing. The children skipped happily after him, heading back home. The Boy and the signpost followed, a little way behind.

There was the Shoe, in its clearing. The Old Woman was sitting slumped unhappily on its doorstep. When she heard the music, she jumped to her feet, beaming.

"There you are!" she cried to the children. "Just in time for supper!"

"Phew!" said the Boy, in relief.

"Very nicely done," said the signpost. "That was a Good Deed, and sometime you will have a reward."

The Boy said sadly, "All I want is Saint George."

"I can tell you where to find Saint George," said a voice, and out from behind a holly bush came a boy. He was about the same age and size as the Magician's Boy, but his face was very round and pale, with a stumpy little nose, and he moved in a stiff sort of way.

"Can you really?" said the Boy, excited. "Please tell me, then!"

"He keeps his horse in our yard," said the round-faced boy.

"Really?" said the Boy. He stared at the other boy. The stumpy nose looked longer than it had been before.

"My father says it's better than a lawn mower," said the round-faced boy, grinning. His nose looked longer still.

The Boy peered more closely, puzzled.

"Then where is Saint George?" he said.

"He'll be coming to pick up his horse at dinnertime," said the round-faced boy, and his nose grew as long as a broomstick.

The signpost made a sudden loud scratchy sound. "Pinocchio," it said, "stop your fibbing!" It jumped up and down on its bouncy little legs, and made the scratchy sound again.

The boy pouted. "Oh Mr. Cricket, you spoil all the fun!" he said, and he stomped off through the wood.

"Was that really Pinocchio?" said the Boy.

"I'm afraid so," said the signpost. "You can't trust him an inch. He just can't resist telling lies, and that nose always gives him away."

"And are you really the Cricket, from Pinocchio's story?"

"I am a signpost," said the signpost with dignity. "I show people the way. It's up to them whether they take it."

He hopped ahead a few paces. "For instance," he said, " just up there you will find a cottage, with a very large beanstalk in its garden."

The Boy ran up the path, and found

himself facing a perfect storybook cottage, with white walls, a thatched roof, and roses climbing round the door. A wisp of smoke rose from a chimney in the roof, and, in the very pretty garden outside the cottage, sure enough, an enormous beanstalk was growing up into the sky.

The Boy ran to the beanstalk and looked up. It was so tall that its top was in the clouds. The stalk was as thick as a tree trunk, and the leaves were as big as umbrellas. He put his foot on the lowest leaf stem. It was flat and strong, like the first rung of a ladder.

"Maybe Saint George is up there," he said.

"If this is Jack's beanstalk, it leads to the Giant's castle, and Saint George might be fighting the Giant. He fights Giants as well as Dragons, and he rescues Fair Maids. I don't much care about the Fair Maids, though."

The signpost said nothing. It just stood there, pointing as usual in two different directions at once.

"I'm going up," said the Boy bravely, and he put his second foot on the second leaf stem of the beanstalk, and began climbing.

six

The Boy went up the beanstalk, one leaf after another. It was very much like climbing a ladder, and a lot easier than climbing a tree.

Partway up, he paused and looked down. The thatched roof of the cottage was just beneath him. Not far away he could see another cottage, with hollyhocks outside the door instead of roses. Walking up the path toward the cottage was a girl. She was wearing a bright red cloak, with a hood pushed halfway back over her long dark hair.

She looked up, smiled at him, and waved. "Hello, Jack!" she called.

The Boy didn't bother to explain that he wasn't Jack. He was looking at her red cloak. He knew who she must be.

He called to her, "Are you going to visit your grandmother?"

"Of course," called the girl. "It's Friday. I've baked her some chocolate chip cookies, they're her favorite."

"Please be careful," the Boy called.

She laughed. "It's just my grandmother! She's in bed!"

The Boy was longing to save her. "No! Listen! It could be a wolf! Make sure her voice isn't deep! Make sure her ears aren't furry! And if she has claws and big sharp teeth, don't stop to say dumb things like 'Oh Grandmama, what big teeth you have'—just run like anything!"

The girl laughed merrily. "You're silly! Have some cookies!" she called, and she swung her arm way back and tossed a little bag up to him.

The Boy caught the bag. "Run! Remember—run!"

"Sure, sure," called Little Red Riding Hood, and off she trotted to her grandmother's cottage.

"She's not listening," said the Boy unhappily, and he went on up the beanstalk. Before long he was so high up that he had a wonderful view over the whole Land of Story, over woods and fields and rivers and high faraway mountains, and beyond them, shining like a lost jewel, the glint of the sea.

Then there was a shaking in the leaves above him, and down the beanstalk came a boy. He was a cheerful-looking boy with a bulging sack slung over his shoulder, and he was whistling. He stopped when he saw the Boy.

"Are you Jack, please?" asked the Boy.

"Of course I am," said Jack. "What are you doing on my beanstalk?"

"I'm looking for Saint George," said the Boy. "I thought he might be chasing your Giant."

"Haven't seen him," said Jack. "I'm going home to my dinner. You be careful if you go up there. I've just pinched a bag of the Giant's treasure, and he's hopping mad. An

angry Giant is not a thing you want to meet."

He grinned at the Boy and went on down the beanstalk.

The Boy looked up through the big green leaves.

"Saint George!" he called. "Are you up there?"

The leaves rustled in the wind, but nobody answered. So the Boy took a deep breath and went on climbing.

At last the leaves grew smaller and he was at the top of the beanstalk, with blue sky above him. Around him was a field of corn.

He looked round at the tall corn plants,

taller than his head. The beanstalk had chosen a very good place to push itself up into the world of the Giant—nobody could notice it here.

But there was no sign of Saint George.

The ground began to shake, as if someone were hitting it with a very big hammer—or walking over it with very big feet. The Boy held his breath, and stood very still, and he heard, coming closer and closer, a huge deep voice.

"Fee fi fo fum," boomed the voice. "I smell the blood of an Englishman!"

And the Giant appeared, tramping through

the cornfield with feet as big as sofas. He was about twenty feet high, with enormous shoulders and a nobbly bald head. He had hair all over his nose, and a third eye in the middle of his forehead. He was a nasty sight, and he was coming closer.

The Boy ran along a row of corn, and out into a grassy field, but the big feet came after him. He looked wildly around. Where could he go? His heart was thumping, thumping, faster than the tramping feet.

He stood still. This was the end. The Giant was going to squish him like a bug.

The thumping feet came closer—and closer—and closer. . . .

SEVEN

Thump, thump, thump, came the Giant's feet.

The Boy stood there shaking.

"Fee fi fo fum," boomed the Giant, really close now. "I smell—"

He stopped suddenly, and his voice dropped to a hopeful whisper.

"—chocolate?"

The Boy couldn't believe what he was hearing. Very fast, he pulled Little Red Riding Hood's bag of chocolate chip cookies out of his pocket.

"Have a cookie, Giant!" he said, and he held one up in the air, reaching as high as he possibly could.

The Giant bent down, a long long way down, and took the cookie between his finger and thumb. It was a big cookie, but in his big hand it looked like a tiny button. The Giant put out his huge purple tongue, which took the cookie into his enormous mouth.

"Mmmmm!" said the Giant happily.

The Boy called up to him, "Please, have you seen Saint George?"

The Giant snorted. "Saint George? That Dragon-chaser? If he came up here, I'd eat him for breakfast!"

"Have another cookie," said the Boy quickly, and held one up. It went away on the tip of the big purple tongue, and the Giant made his happy noise again. It seemed to the Boy a very good time to leave, before the Giant might get cross again.

"Here, have all of them!" he said, and he

emptied the bag of chocolate chip cookies into the grass. With a great crash the Giant went down on his hands and knees, and while he was trying to pick up the cookies with his big clumsy fingers, the Boy ran back into the cornfield, found the beanstalk, and began climbing down.

He went down from leaf stem to leaf stem, much faster than he had come up. Down, down, down, he went. He was so pleased to be getting away from the Giant that he didn't look where he was going—until there was a terrible snarling roar below him, and he felt a great tug at the bottom of one leg of his jeans.

He looked down. A huge wolf was there, right under his feet at the bottom of the beanstalk. It spat out a piece of the Boy's jeans and turned to jump up again. The Boy hastily climbed back up several leaf stems, and held on tight.

Snarling, the wolf leaped at him, snapping its jaws. Its teeth looked very big and very sharp.

"You warned her, you little weasel!" howled the wolf. "You told her! And she ran!"

The Boy was delighted. "Good for her!" he said.

The wolf snarled with fury. "You spoiled everything! The wolf wants to *eat* Red Riding Hood!"

"Not this time!" said the Boy. He held tightly to the beanstalk, as the wolf leaped up at him again, biting at the air.

"I'll eat you instead!" the wolf hissed. "I can wait!"

It lay down at the bottom of the beanstalk, panting. Its long red tongue hung out over its sharp white teeth, and its bright eyes glared up at the Boy.

The Boy sat down on a leaf stem. Now he was scared. He called out, "Saint George, where are you? Come and help me!"

But nobody came.

The wolf lay there looking up at the Boy, showing its teeth. Once in a while it gave a nasty growl.

"Dinnertime," it said, and licked its lips.

The Boy didn't want to be dinner. The leaf stem was sticking into his leg, and his foot was going to sleep. He kept tight hold of the edge of a leaf, to make sure he didn't fall off. What ever was he to do?

He turned his head to look around, and a

cluster of bean pods poked him in the eye.

"Ow!" the Boy said.

Then he had an idea.

A very good idea.

EIGHT

The enormous beanstalk was covered not only with leaves but with bright red flowers and long bean pods. Some of the pods were very fat. They were starting to dry out, and they were nearly ready to pop.

The Boy often had to pick peas and beans in the Magician's garden, so he knew that the beans in those dry pods would be hard as stones. And because this beanstalk was so huge, the beans would also be ten times the size of a regular bean.

He reached up to the nearest dry bean pod, which was as long as his arm. It was far too big and hard for him to pick it, but perhaps he could squeeze it hard enough to make it pop open. He put both his arms round the end of the pod and hugged it, hard—and it opened.

There inside lay six hard round green beans. They were even bigger than he expected.

The Boy pulled out a bean, the size of a baseball. He aimed very carefully, and he threw it at the wolf.

"Ow!" The wolf jumped up in the

air, as the bean hit it on the back.

The Boy grinned. He threw another giant bean, and it hit the wolf full on the nose. The wolf screeched. Then it backed away from the Boy and howled in rage.

The door of Jack's cottage swung open and Jack came running out. He was still chewing his dinner, and he had a chunk of bread in his hand. He stared at the wolf, and then up at the Boy.

"Wolf," he said, "what are you doing under my beanstalk? Go back to your own story!"

The wolf snarled at him.

"Go on," Jack said sternly. "You know the rules."

The wolf bared its teeth, which looked bigger and sharper than ever. "It was him," it said sulkily. "*He* broke the rules. He warned Red Riding Hood to watch out for me."

"He doesn't know any better," said Jack. "He's a visitor, he's on a quest. *You* belong here. Go home! Go on!"

"No fair," said the wolf. He looked at the Boy, and bared his teeth again.

"If you're not careful I'll bring my Giant down here," Jack said. "Wolves are his favorite thing for dinner, if he can't catch boys."

The wolf whined. "No fair," it said, but it slunk off with its tail between its legs.

"Thanks very much," said the Boy to

Jack. He climbed down off the beanstalk. "What's a quest?"

"Looking for something," Jack said. "Or someone. You're on a quest to find Saint George."

"And I'm no good at it," said the Boy gloomily.

"Cheer up," said Jack. "Here, have a snack." He held out his piece of bread.

"Thanks!" said the Boy. He took a bite. It was very good bread.

Jack said, "If Saint George is here, he's in his own story. Everyone is. And his story is 'Saint George and the Dragon,' right?"

"Right," said the Boy, chewing.

"Try looking for the Dragon. Dragons are hard to miss. Then you'll find Saint George with him!"

"That's a great idea," the Boy said.

"Good luck!" said Jack. "I'm off to bother my Giant again." He slapped the Boy on the back, and began climbing up the beanstalk.

"He loves chocolate!" the Boy called after him.

But Jack was gone.

NINE

A gruff voice said, "So now you're looking for a Dragon?"

The Boy looked down. It was the signpost, standing there pointing as usual in both directions.

"Where have you been?" the Boy said. He took another bite of bread.

"Right here," said the signpost. "I can't climb beanstalks, and wolves don't eat signposts. Don't eat that last bit of bread."

The Boy was about to pop it in his mouth, but he stopped. "Are you hungry?" he said.

"Signposts don't eat, stupid," said the signpost. "Share it with the birds. They might be useful."

The Boy broke his last bit of bread into crumbs, and scattered them on the ground. At once, four and twenty blackbirds came swooping down out of the trees and the beanstalk and pecked them up.

The Boy looked at them, and remembered.

"You be careful!" he said. "Someone wants to catch all of you, and bake you in a pie!"

"Oh, that's okay," said the biggest blackbird. "It's just the Magician. He doesn't really cook us. We just sit in this big dish and he puts a baked crust over us. People think they have a yummy pie to eat, but when they cut it, we all fly out, singing. You should see their faces!"

"I know a Magician like that," said the Boy.

"Thanks for the crumbs," said the blackbird. She looked at him with her head on one side. "You need any bird help?"

"Yes please," said the Boy. "Will you tell me if you can see any parts of the wood where the trees have been burned by fire?"

"Fire?" said the bird.

"I'm looking for a Dragon," said the Boy. "Dragons breathe fire all the time, they can't help it."

"Okay," said the biggest blackbird. She whistled to the others, and all twenty-four of them flew up past the treetops and disappeared.

The Boy looked at the signpost with respect.

"The birds were a good idea," he said.

"Well, I *am* supposed to show people the way," said the signpost. "You just have to choose which one."

The birds came flying down again like a fall of black snow. They saluted.

"Burned trees two miles east, sir," said one.

"Black treetops one mile north, sir," said another.

"Black trees five hundred yards south, sir," said a third.

"Burned trees a hundred yards west, sir," said the biggest blackbird, "and still smoking!"

"That's it!" said the Boy. "The Dragon must be still there! Let's go west!"

He looked up to see which way the sun was shining. "This way!" he said, and they all set off. The blackbirds fluttered from tree to tree, singing.

TEN

Soon the Boy could smell smoke. He ran through the trees, and he thought he saw the tip of an enormous tail disappearing ahead of him. Then he began to hear voices calling. Frightened voices.

"Help!" cried the first voice.

"Help, help!" cried the second.

"Save us!" called the third.

Suddenly the Boy was out in a grassy clearing. A wide strip of the grass was burned black, still smoking, and blackened leaves hung from the lower branches of the trees on the other side.

It was a very big clearing, the size of a football field.

The signpost stumped out after the Boy and stood next to him, looking round.

The frightened shouts grew louder, and then out of the trees on the left side of the clearing three figures came running. The Boy recognized them; they were the people dressed like the puppets from his play. There was the fat round figure of Father Christmas, the Doctor in his dark coat, and the Turkish Knight with his bright baggy pants flapping.

"Help!" they cried as they ran. "Save us!"

And after them came the Dragon.

He was a huge, handsome Dragon, bright green all over, with red eyes and golden claws. Smoke and flame flew out of his nostrils when he opened his great red jaws to roar.

"Wow!" said the signpost.

The Turkish Knight turned bravely to fight the Dragon, waving his curved sword.

But the Dragon swung his long scaly neck sideways, and the side of his bony green head knocked the Turkish Knight off his feet and up into the air.

"*Waaaaah!*" cried the Turkish Knight, and he flew through the air and into the branches of a big oak tree, where he stuck, upside down.

The Dragon galloped over to the tree and started trying to climb it.

The Boy was watching wide-eyed. "Saint George *must* be here now!" he said.

"Oh yes," said the signpost. "He certainly is."

"Saint George!" called the poor upside-down Turkish Knight. "Help!"

"Saint George!" called the Doctor, dodging in and out of the trees.

The Dragon was too big to climb the tree. He snarled up at the Turkish Knight, showing his enormous white teeth.

"Saint George!" called the Boy. "Where are you, Saint George?"

He looked all round him, at the smoking grass and the blackened leaves.

Then very slowly, one by one, out into the clearing, from behind every tree and bush, came all the people he had met in the Land of Story. The Old Woman was there, with all her children around her, and the Pied Piper, carrying his pipe.

Little Zoe waved to the Boy. Red Riding Hood was there, with the wolf slinking sulkily behind her. Jack came out onto the sooty grass, and the big head of the Giant popped up behind a tree and looked down at the Boy. Pinocchio moved out stiffly, his nose a normal size now. And around them all the four and twenty blackbirds swooped and fluttered, singing.

And every single person and creature was looking at the Boy.

The Boy stared at them all. What were they doing? The Dragon would eat them!

"Saint George!" he shouted urgently.

Out of the crowd of people, Father Christmas walked forward toward the Boy, and everyone turned to watch. The old man was carrying a white tunic with a big red cross on it, and a sword, and a small round shield.

He stopped in front of the Boy, and put the tunic over the Boy's astonished head.

Then he put the sword into the Boy's right hand, and the shield into his left.

The signpost said softly:

"Only a child can find the way
To bring Saint George back to the play."

The Boy said, "But I'm not Saint George!"

"You are now," the signpost said.

ELEVEN

Everyone in the clearing shouted and cheered. "Saint George!" they cried. "Hurray for Saint George!"

The Boy looked down at his tunic. It was certainly the right uniform for Saint George. He took a deep breath, and he thrust his sword up into the air and waved it.

Everyone cheered even louder.

"Dragon!" shouted the Boy. "I challenge you to fight!"

The Dragon was busily thumping his tail against the oak tree, trying to shake the Turkish Knight out of it. He looked up and saw the Boy, and gave a great angry roar. Fire shot out of his nostrils and burned some more grass.

"Go home, peanut!" roared the Dragon. "Don't bother me!"

He turned back to the Turkish Knight, and puffed a cloud of smoke up at him. The Turkish Knight squealed, and began to cough.

The Boy wasn't about to be called a peanut, especially now that he was Saint George. He moved quietly toward the Dragon, reached past one of the great golden claws, and jabbed the tip of his sword into the Dragon's toe.

"Ow!" said the Dragon, and the Boy jumped back very fast before the big claw could grab at him.

"Fight, Dragon!" he shouted bravely.

"RRRROOOOOOAAAAAWWWW!" roared the Dragon, and all the blackbirds flew up into the sky in alarm. Everyone in the watching crowd moved one step backward, but they also began to cheer and shout.

"Come on, Saint George!" shouted Jack.

"Yay, Saint George!" yelled the Old Woman's children.

"Boo to the Dragon!" called Red Riding Hood.

The Dragon snarled, and scuffed at the ground with one huge front claw. He put his head down and rushed full tilt at the Boy, roaring as he came.

The Boy held up his shield and jumped sideways, just as the great red jaws were about to swallow him up. The Dragon's head hit the shield and sent the Boy rolling head over heels across the clearing. His shield clanged like a bell as it bounced away over the ground, and his sword went flying. But he managed to snatch up the sword before the Dragon could turn to charge again.

The Dragon huffed out a ball of fire, and the Boy dodged. He felt the flames singe the hair above his ear.

"RRRROOOOOOAAAAAWWWW!" roared the Dragon again, and he brought his enormous green tail swinging round from behind to knock the Boy off his feet.

"Jump, Saint George!" called Pinocchio.

Just in time, the Boy jumped up into the

air, and the tail swished by underneath him. It was swishing so fast that it made the Dragon swing round in a circle, staggering to keep his balance.

"Boo, mean old Dragon!" shouted the Old Woman's children. "BOO!"

The Dragon snarled and blew smoke at them.

The Boy stood tall, facing the Dragon. He had no shield now, but he held his sword firmly in front of him. "Come on, Dragon!" he yelled. "Come and fight!"

The Dragon's eyes were gleaming like red stars. He stood there green and furious, making a hissing sound like a huge angry cat.

And then he charged.

He thundered across the clearing toward the Boy, roaring, and the ground shook, and the people of the Land of Story gazed in horror as he came. The sunlight flashed from the Dragon's golden claws and the long white teeth in his dreadful gaping mouth.

The Boy stood there watching, waiting. He wanted to run. He was going to be killed!

But he knew he had to be Saint George. So as the enormous green Dragon came rushing toward him, with the flashing gold claws on either side, and the terrible open jaws above, he didn't move. He stood there still and firm, with his sword held straight out in front of him.

And the Dragon ran right onto the sword, and it went into his chest, right up to the hilt. The Boy let go just in time, and dodged aside. The Dragon staggered to a halt, and let out a great shriek. Everyone in the clearing cheered and shouted and jumped up and down.

The Boy darted forward and pulled out his sword and held it up high. Everyone cheered again.

Just for a moment, something puzzled the Boy. He couldn't see any blood on the Dragon's chest, and his sword seemed to have gone in and come out very easily, as if it had been stuck into a sofa, or a stuffed toy.

But the Boy didn't have any more time to think, because the Dragon had begun to die a most spectacular death. He staggered across the blackened grass, roaring, and the cheering crowd scattered out of his way. He blew an angry puff of smoke at them.

He staggered round in a circle, and gave another tremendous roar.

Then he fell over, and lay on his side. He let out three perfectly round puffs of smoke and they drifted up to the sky. The Dragon roared, more weakly. His tail thrashed to and fro over the grass.

The people in the crowd were cheering even more loudly. "Hurray for Saint George!" they shouted. "Saint George is the champion!"

The Boy waved his sword in the air. As he did it, he remembered that this was exactly what he had always made the Saint George puppet do, in his own world, when he was working the puppet play.

And he realized that the Dragon was doing exactly the same things he himself had made the puppet dragon do, when it was dying. He had always ended by having the puppet dragon heave itself up off the ground with a final terrifying roar, before falling down dead. The children in the audience had always loved that.

He moved out into the center of the clearing, and looked at the Dragon.

The Dragon thrashed his tail about some more, and then he lifted his whole body up off the ground with a huge terrifying roar— and he fell down dead.

But he grinned at the Boy as he did it, and before he closed his eyes, he *winked*.

TWELVE

The Boy stared at the dead Dragon.

All around him, people were cheering and hooting and whistling. The signpost was jumping up and down on its chunky little legs, shouting, "Well done! Well done!" The Pied Piper was playing a victory march on his pipe. All the Old Woman's children were laughing and waving, and

Jack was dancing a happy jig with Red Riding Hood.

The four and twenty blackbirds were darting to and fro round the Boy's head, singing. Their song grew louder and louder, and they flew closer and closer, so that he could see nothing but a whirl of black feathers. Then he felt as if they were picking him up to fly with them, carrying him up, up, up, high above the trees. . . .

And suddenly the Boy was standing behind the puppet theatre, holding puppet strings in his hands, and below him on the stage was the still shape of a little green dragon, with a little Saint George, in his white tunic with the red cross on it, waving his sword triumphantly in the air.

In a corner of the stage was a tiny signpost, its arms pointing in two directions. There were no strings attached to the signpost, but for a moment the Boy thought he saw one of its arms wave to him. He blinked.

All around him were the children at Mr. Pennywinkle's party, cheering and clapping their hands. "Hooray!" they shouted. "Good old Saint George! He won!"

A big hand took hold of the Boy's shoulder. He looked up.

It was the Magician, gazing down at him with his dark mysterious eyes.

"Come and take a bow, puppet master," he said.

The Boy let go of the strings and came out from behind the little theatre. The Magician took his hand, and the children shouted and cheered while they both bowed, again and again.

The Magician said in the Boy's ear, over the sound of the cheers, "Well done. Very well done."

"I didn't think I could possibly be Saint George," the Boy said.

"I know you didn't," said the Magician. "But you were, weren't you? I shall stop calling you 'Boy' now. I shall call you 'George,' to remind you."

The Boy looked up again, into the dark eyes under the shaggy dark eyebrows. "Thank you," he said. He took a deep breath. "And please, will you teach me magic?"

The Magician smiled. "Of course I will," he said. "The time is right, now. We shall start your lessons tomorrow, George."

And so they did.

• • •

ALADDIN PAPERBACKS

An imprint of Simon & Schuster Children's Publishing Division

1230 Avenue of the Americas, New York, NY 10020

Text copyright © 2005 by Susan Cooper

Illustrations copyright © 2005 by Serena Riglietti

All rights reserved, including the right of reproduction in whole or in part in any form.

ALADDIN PAPERBACKS and colophon are trademarks of Simon & Schuster, Inc.

Also available in a Margaret K. McElderry Books hardcover edition.

Designed by Ann Bobco

The text of this book was set in Times New Roman.

The illustrations for this book were rendered in pen and ink, watercolor, and colored pencils.

Manufactured in the United States of America

First Aladdin Paperbacks edition June 2006

10   9

The Library of Congress has cataloged the hardcover edition as follows:

Cooper, Susan, 1935–

The magician's boy / Susan Cooper

p. cm.

Summary: A Boy who works for a Magician meets familiar fairy-tale characters when he is transported to the Land of Story in search of a missing puppet.

ISBN-13: 978-0-689-87622-6 (hc.)

ISBN-10: 0-689-87622-X (hc.)

[1. Fairy tales. 2. Characters in literature—Fiction. 3. Puppets—Fiction.
4. Puppet theater—Fiction. 5. Magicians—Fiction.] I. Title.

PZ8.C7926Mag 2005

[Fic]—dc22

2004008549

ISBN-13: 978-1-4169-1555-3 (Aladdin pbk.)

ISBN-10: 1-4169-1555-9 (Aladdin pbk.)

0311 FFG